CONTENTS

DEDICATION

My thanks and appreciation to
Ide, Celine and Lynn,
who exercised their considerable talents
in transforming my story into this book.

CHARLIE WANTS A BIKE

'Dad, I'd like a bike,' Charlie Harte said to his dad.

'I know, Charlie, son,' Dad said, 'but I can't afford it.'

Charlie didn't say: Ah, please, Dad! Why can't I have a bike?

He knew they had no money. Dad lost his job when the factory closed. So, the Hartes were hard up.

Charlie was sad. He didn't care about having no money, but he would really love a bike.

Most of the children in his street had bikes. They rode them up and down past Charlie's house.

Paul Watson had a brand new racing bike, and he could do tricks. He could sit on the handlebars and cycle backwards.

Charlie would love to try that.

One morning Charlie got up very early. The birds had only just begun to sing. Charlie was going to the fields outside the town to pick mushrooms. He had to go early. If he didn't, the other pickers would be there before him, and all the good ones would be gone.

The town was dead. Charlie was alone in the street. Morgan's dog was the only thing that moved. He was sniffing at a dustbin.

The bins and bags of rubbish were sitting on the footpaths. They had been there all night. They were lining the edges of the footpaths like a crowd of people waiting to watch a parade.

Before one house an old, rusted bike frame stood on its end between two bins. It was a useless thing, fit only for the dump, but Charlie's head buzzed with an idea.

Would it be OK if he took the bike frame? It wouldn't be stealing. After all, the people had put it out there to send it to the dump.

But he knew he shouldn't take it without asking. His mam and dad were very strict about things like that. Mam often said to him, 'Remember, Charlie, always be sure you know the difference between what's yours and what isn't yours.'

He would have to ask the people for the frame, so he knocked at the door. The knock sounded very loud in the quiet street.

Nobody answered.

Charlie knocked again, louder this time. Still no answer.

He knocked again, a good bang.

An upstairs window opened, and a head came out. It was a woman's head, and her hair was all tossed from the bed. Her eyes were half-closed with sleep, and the sides of her mouth were turned down. Charlie could see that she was cross.

'What's all this racket about at this hour of the morning?' the woman shouted.

'It's only me, Missus,' said Charlie.

'And who are you?' the woman asked, and Charlie could hear the anger ringing in her voice.

'Charlie Harte, Missus,' he said.

'And what do you want, Charlie Harte?' she barked.

'Can I have the old bike frame, please, Missus?' he asked.

'Oh, take it away with you, and don't ever again knock at my door before the shops open.'

'Thanks, Missus,' said Charlie.

Charlie forgot that he was on his way to pick mushrooms. He took the frame and put it across his shoulders. He ran all the way home.

SMALL BEGINNINGS

Mam and Dad were still in bed when he got home. They were sound asleep, but they woke up when they heard Charlie shouting downstairs.

'Mam. Dad,' he was shouting, 'I have a bike.

They came downstairs in their pyjamas.

'What are you shouting about?' Mam said. 'That's not a bike.'

'You've only got an old rusty frame there,' Dad said. 'Where's the saddle, and the wheels and all the rest of it?'

'I know the other bits are missing,' Charlie said, 'but I might get them yet.'

'And where do you think you could get them, Charlie?' Mam said.

'I don't know,' Charlie said. 'Maybe I

could go out early on a few bin mornings and pick them up around the town.'

'Don't be daft,' Dad said. 'People throw things away only when they're no good.'

Next day Charlie decided to do something about the bike. He went to Garvey's bike shop.

'Have you any old wheels or saddles?' he asked the man in the shop.

'No, we don't keep old stuff,' the man said. 'But why don't you try Moone's second-hand shop around the corner? They have a lot of second-hand bikes and parts.'

'Thank you very much, Mister,' Charlie said. 'I'll try Moone's.'

Charlie went around the corner to Moone's.

'Any old bike parts?' he asked Mr Moone.

'Yes, we have lots of parts,' Mr Moone said. 'What part do you want?'

'I have no money,' Charlie said.

Mr Moone laughed. 'Ha-ha-ha! No money! Money is very handy when you want to buy something, isn't it, young man? No money! Ha-ha-ha!'

'I thought you might have something you want to throw away,' Charlie said. 'You know, like something you might be sending to the dump.'

'What you should do is go down to the end of the street to Flanagan's scrapyard,' Mr Moone said.

'Thanks, Mr Moone. I'll do that,' said Charlie.

THE SCRAPHEAP

Flanagan's yard was huge, and it was most untidy. It was cluttered with old cars and vans, prams, washing machines, cookers, sewing machines and tractors. Beside them were heaps of rusting and broken metal parts in piles rising up as high as houses.

Little paths wound in and around the heaps of scrap. Charlie didn't know where to start to look for bike parts.

He could not see anybody to ask, but there was a hut just inside the gate. Charlie went to the hut and knocked at the door.

'Come in,' a voice said.

Charlie went in. A man with dirty clothes, stained with grease, sat at a desk. His face was black with oil. His eyes looked very white in the black.

'What do you want, little boy?' he growled. He sounded like a watchdog.

'I'm looking for Mr Flanagan,' Charlie said.

'Well, you've found him,' the man said, and he smiled a white toothy smile in his black face. 'Now tell me what you want.'

'Bike parts, Mr Flanagan,' Charlie said, and he went on, 'I have a frame and I want parts to make a bike.'

'Come with me,' said Miko Flanagan, and he stood up.

He led Charlie along the narrow paths through the scrap.

'Where did you get all that stuff?' Charlie asked.

'I buy old cars and things,' Miko said. 'I'll buy any kind of machine. Then I take them asunder, and I sell any part that's OK. I love doing that. It's great to see something new growing out of old bangers.'

He took Charlie to a corner of the yard that he called his bicycle nest.

'There you go,' he said. 'All the bike parts are there. See what you can find.'

Bicycle parts were heaped together in a great pile in the corner.

When Miko had gone back to the hut, Charlie began to search through the pile. It was hard to pull things out from the bottom, so he climbed up to the top.

It wasn't easy to find a place to stand, but Charlie managed somehow. He began to pull things out – bits of mudguards, tail-lights, handlebars.

Most of the things were of no use to him. But he found a perfect wheel and then another. Later he came across two complete mudguards and a tail-light.

Charlie brought the mudguards, two wheels, and tail-light to the hut.

'I found these, Mr Flanagan,' he said.

'You won't build much of a bike with those,' Miko said. 'You have two front wheels!'

MIKO TO THE RESCUE

Miko went back to the bicycle nest with Charlie. He was a very strong man, and he flung things aside until he got into the centre of the pile. He was lost from sight, but Charlie could hear him rummaging among the scrap. Whole bikes and parts of bikes went flying to the top of the heap, and Charlie had to stand well back as some pieces landed near him on the path.

'A good scrapyard man knows where to look,' Miko shouted.

He went on searching for a while, and then he came out with a back wheel, a saddle, a chain-wheel, pedals, a chain, brakes, and a bell.

'Now you have the makings of a bike,' he said.

'I can't take them, Mr Flanagan,' Charlie said.

'I suppose there's too much there for you to carry,' Miko said.

'No,' said Charlie. 'That's not it.'

'All right,' Miko said. 'Tell me where you live. I'll take them for you in the van when I finish here this evening.'

'I'm sorry, Mr Flanagan,' Charlie said, 'but I have no money. I can't pay for those things.'

Miko stopped and scratched his head. 'First of all you must stop calling me Mr Flanagan. My name is Miko.'

'All right, Miko,' Charlie said.

'Were you listening to me,' Miko said, 'when I said I loved seeing things being made out of old scrap? That's more important to me than money.'

'Yes, Miko,' Charlie said.

'Right. Now, you can have those parts

free of charge if you promise me something. Promise me that you'll show me the bike when you've made it.'

Charlie promised.

* * *

After tea Miko's van pulled up outside Charlie's house. Miko began to unload the bike parts and lay them on the footpath.

'Where is that man going with that stuff?' Mam asked. 'Haven't we got enough rubbish in the house already?'

'That's not rubbish,' Charlie said. 'That's the stuff for my new bike.'

'What new bike?' said Mam. 'You don't mean to tell me you're going to make a bike out of that! You're daft!'

'I was hoping Dad might help me,' Charlie said.

'I'm sure he will,' Mam said, 'because he's

daft too. Anyway, I don't want to see that rubbish cluttering up my house.'

'It's OK,' Dad said. 'We'll take them out to the shed. They won't be in your way there.'

CHARLIE'S BIKE

Dad was good at fixing things. He got out his spanners and screwdrivers and got to work on the bike.

Some nuts and bolts were needed, and Charlie went back to the scrapyard to see if he could find any. Miko gave him a bag of nuts and bolts of different sizes.

Dad and Charlie worked at the bike for two days. Dad did most of the work, but Charlie watched every move he made.

At last the bike was ready. It had an old-fashioned look about it. The frame was thick and heavy, and the handlebars were high and wide. It was a bit like Miss Hannon's old high nelly. But it *was* a bike!

'There you go,' Dad said. 'Try it out.'

Charlie wheeled the rusty old bike out to

the street. Dad sat on the window sill to watch.

The bike creaked and squeaked, but Charlie got up on it and rode it down the street. It wasn't a fast bike, because it was old, but Charlie was delighted with it. At last he had a bike of his very own.

He turned at the top of the street and rode it back again. Peter Mills flew past him on his flashy new bike. As he passed Charlie, he rang his bell, ting-a-ling-a-ling-a-ling.

Charlie knew Peter rang the bell just to mock his home-made bike.

When Peter was on the way back, he shouted, 'Hi, Charlie, where did you get the old boneshaker?'

Charlie ignored him.

'It's fine,' he told his dad when he got back. 'It's a bit slow, and it squeaks a bit, but it's OK.'

'Ride it around for a few days,' Dad said. 'Give it a chance to loosen out. The parts aren't used to each other yet.'

Other children in the street called it names, like 'Squeaker', and 'Banger', and 'Hobby Horse'.

But Charlie didn't mind. He had a bike. He rode it around the town.

Then he rode it to the scrapyard to show it to Miko Flanagan.

Miko came out of the hut. 'I heard you coming,' he said. 'I heard that thing squeaking as soon as you turned in the gate. Here, let me oil it for you.'

Miko got an oiling can, and he oiled all the moving parts.

'Try it now,' he said.

Charlie rode the bike around the scrapyard, and it didn't make a sound. If you weren't looking at it, you wouldn't know it was on the move.

Charlie told his best friends in the school about his bike. They came home with him one day to see it.

'It looks a bit shabby,' said Minnie. 'I mean with the rust and all.'

'I know,' Charlie said. 'It needs a lick of paint.'

'We have some paint at home,' said Kate.

'So have we,' said Andy.

'We have some too,' said Minnie, 'but you must clean off the rust first. I'll get some sandpaper.'

They got the sandpaper and the paints and brought them to Charlie's house.

First of all they scraped off all the rust with the sandpaper. Then they painted the bike. Charlie did most of it.

He painted it black and white and yellow. He put the colour on in stripes along the frame of the bike.

'It's like a tiger,' said Kate.

'That's what I'll call it,' said Charlie. 'From now on its name is Tiger!'

Even though the bike was old and didn't move fast, Charlie came to love it.

The first thing he did every morning when he got up was go out to see Tiger, his bike of many colours.

Charlie talked to the bike.

'Good morning, Tiger,' he said. 'I hope you're feeling well this morning.'

Charlie rode the bike everywhere. He rode it to school, to the shop, to the sports field.

'Next thing you'll be taking that old bike to bed with you,' his mam said.

Charlie rode the bike to school every morning, and home again in the afternoon.

At school he put Tiger in the shed with the other bikes. Most of the others were new and shining, but they all looked the same.

'What about the bike race?' Kate asked him. 'You must go in the bike race too.'

'Go on, Charlie. Have a go,' Andy said. 'You might win.'

'I don't want to give them the chance to laugh at Tiger, if we come last,' Charlie said.

'Who cares if they laugh,' Kate said. 'They laugh because they're jealous. They have only ordinary bikes.'

'All right,' said Charlie. 'I'll give it a try.'

Every day Charlie went out practising on his bike. He rode it on the grass of the green near his house. He wanted to get used to riding on grass to be ready for the sports field.

But when Thursday came, he didn't want to go in the bike race. He knew he hadn't a chance. Tiger always went at his own pace, and Charlie couldn't make him hurry.

But Kate and Minnie and Andy kept at him, and, in the end, he gave his name to

Mr Brown for the sack race and the bike race.

Friday was a sunny day, and the whole school went up to the sports field. Parents and friends were there too.

'Cheer up, Charlie,' Andy said. 'You might win.'

'Not the bike race,' Charlie said. 'I don't think Tiger can win. He's not a racing bike.'

Andy came second in the egg-and-spoon race, and Kate and Minnie were last in the three-legged race. Charlie came second in the sack race, but there was no prize for second.

THE RACE

The bike race was to be the last of all. Charlie got fed up of waiting, so he rode his bike up and down the field to get ready.

At long last Mr Brown called out: 'Girls and boys for the bike race please come to the start.'

Ten bikes went to the start. Mr Brown made them line up behind a rope. Charlie was in the centre. He had one foot on a pedal and the other on the ground, ready to push.

Then Mr Brown said, 'Ready, steady, go!'

They started and rode down the field as if a herd of wild bulls was chasing them.

Most of the bikes were new, and they went very fast.

Charlie was up with the others for the first

part of the race, but then he began to fall behind.

Soon he was last. He could see the others going away from him, but he kept on trying.

He tried as hard as he could, but it was no use. The bike was too old and too heavy, and poor old Tiger came last.

Peter Mills won the bike race. When he crossed the line, he jumped down off the bike and looked at the people watching. He had a big smile on his face, and he waved at his mother.

Charlie was last across the line. Mr Brown said, 'Good try, Charlie!'

Charlie hated it when people said things like that to him, having pity on him.

He said nothing to Mr Brown, just wheeled the bike back to his friends, and sat down.

'Coming last is not very nice,' Charlie said to his friends.

Miss Power was passing, and she heard him.

'Never mind, Charlie,' she said. 'You have a very nice bike. I love the colours.'

'Thanks,' said Charlie.

'Don't be so sad, Charlie,' Minnie said to him. 'Tiger is not a racing bike.'

'That's right,' Andy said. 'I'll bet Peter Mills's bike wouldn't last very long on a rough road.'

'Tiger is strong, not fast,' said Kate.

Charlie just sat there, saying nothing.

Then the sports were over, and it was time to give the prizes.

Mr Brown made a speech, but nobody was listening. Miss Power was standing beside him, and her job was to read the names of the winners from a notebook.

Charlie stood at the back of the crowd with Kate and Minnie and Andy.

Miss Power read out the names of the

winners, and each one went up in turn to the stand. Mr Brown smiled and shook their hands and gave them their prizes.

The people clapped each prize-winner. Charlie clapped too, but he was hoping it would end soon, so that he could go home.

After the prize-giving Mr Brown made a speech thanking everyone who helped to run the sports.

While he was talking, Charlie slipped away and walked home alone. He didn't ride Tiger. 'It wouldn't be right,' he said to himself. 'Both Tiger and I have been insulted today. He isn't a good bike; I'm not a good rider. So, we'll walk home and be sad together.'

A WALKMAN

Charlie and Miko became great friends.
Charlie called to the scrapyard almost every
day on his way home from school.

'Anything new today?' he would ask.

'Yeah,' Miko would say. 'Got in a 1973
Mini. A very good gear box and clutch.' Or
he might say, 'Nothing much today. Just an
old Bendix washing machine on its last legs,
but the motor isn't too bad.'

Then one day Miko said, 'Found
something in an old Ford Anglia that came
in today. Here, you might like it.'

He handed Charlie a walkman radio. It
was old, stained and shabby.

'Does it work, Miko?'

'Yes. It just needed a battery.'

'Why did they throw it away then?'

'Maybe because it got shabby,' Miko said. 'It's not enough for some people to have a thing that works; it must be all bright and shiny as well.'

Charlie tried the walkman. There was a DJ talking on the radio and Charlie could hear him as if he were standing two feet away. Then the music started. It was brilliant! Charlie was thrilled.

'Hey!' he said. 'Miko, this is fantastic!'

The radio had a clip to attach it to his belt or the waistband of his jeans.

When Charlie got home, he got his dad's hammer and changed the clip. He bent it around the handlebars of the bike. He preferred to have it there than clipped on to his jeans.

Then he went for a ride up and down the street. He put the headphones on and listened to music. It clanged in his ears. It was bliss!

Charlie passed by Peter Mills on the street. He saw Peter's mouth making shout sounds, but he couldn't hear over the noise of the Ragged Robins banging out their latest single.

WHO'S THERE?

Charlie smiled when he saw the other children in the street eyeing him with envy as he rode up and down, listening to his walkman.

Then someone said, 'Charlie, you're an ass.'

He pulled the headphones from his ears and shouted, 'Who said that?'

Nobody answered. The children who were near him looked at each other and at him. They didn't seem to know what he was talking about. Peter Mills and others were too far away, and they were not looking in his direction anyway.

Charlie put the headphones back on and got on the bike again. As soon as he began pushing on the pedals, the voice spoke:

'You're still an ass.'

Again Charlie took off the headphones and looked around. The children in the street had lost interest in him and his walkman.

Nobody was looking in his direction. It was scary.

Charlie put the headphones on again. Nothing happened. He was relieved, and he got on the bike. He nearly fell off when the voice spoke again: 'How many times do I have to tell you that you're an ass?'

It was a funny voice, a bit like his Uncle Ted's voice on the phone. Must be some stunt by the radio people, he thought and he continued his ride towards the end of the street.

'Don't ignore me, Charlie Harte,' said the voice. Charlie stayed on the bike, but he pulled off the headphones and looked around. Nobody in the street had spoken.

He was sure of that.

He put the headphones on again and rode back the other way. 'Did you hear me, Charlie?' came the voice.

'Who the hell are you?' Charlie said to the air. There was nothing else to say it to.

'I'm Tiger,' said the voice. 'I'm your bike.'

'Hump off!' Charlie said. 'Bikes don't talk.'

'This bike does, Charlie. Once you put that metal clip on my handlebars. I was able to send my sound waves through those wires and make words to echo in your ears.'

'I don't believe it.'

'It's true. I couldn't talk to everyone, mind you. Just you.'

'Why just me?'

'Everything about you is just right, your weight on the saddle, the bones of your right foot, the twists and turns round your ear-hole, the dance of your brain waves when you think; everything is right.'

'Why do you want to talk to me? You frightened the life out of me!' Charlie complained.

'You, Charlie, are my dear friend. You are the one who pulled me out of that scrapheap and arranged for all those transplants that brought me back to life. I am your child. I love you, Charlie.'

'Give over!' Charlie said. 'That old soppy stuff makes me sick.'

'Okay, then, tough man Charlie, love and that kind of thing is out. But I am your friend forever.'

'Nice friend!'

'I think, Charlie, you mean that in a mocking way.'

'Bloody sure I do. You put the heart crosswise in me, and, as well as that, you called me an ass.'

'I call you an ass for your own good. Do you know how dangerous it is to ride around on a bike like me and have your ears full of that crazy Ragged Robins music? You're not able to hear the thunder of heavy traffic around you.'

'I can see.'

'You can't see out the back of your head.'

Charlie was silent for a moment. 'Does that mean I can't listen to the radio when I'm riding the bike?'

'It does. But, when you're off the bike, put the headphones on and talk to me from time to time. I can be of great help to you.'

'How?'

'I am not your ordinary bike, Charlie. I am the Supergeist of the bicycle world. I know the secrets of the universe, what has been and what is to come.'

CHARLIE IN BUSINESS

Life changed for Charlie. He had a chat with Tiger every morning and evening, and sometimes during the day as well. He shared his troubles and joys with his beloved bike.

One evening Tiger aired one of his own problems.

'Charlie,' he began, 'I don't know how to say this to you, but my back tyre is not so good. You're a bit hard on the brakes you know.'

'Can't do anything about it now, Tiger. No funds!'

'Try Miko,' the bike urged. 'Anyway, you should be doing something not to be always short of cash. You shouldn't leave it all to your dad and your mam.'

'What could I do?'

'Try setting up a courier service.'

'A what?'

'Doing messages for people and getting paid for it. Get your dad to hang a plate under my crossbar and print the name of your company on it.'

Two days later Charlie wheeled out the bike with a new tin plate hanging from the crossbar. Printed on the plate were the words CH Courier Service.

At first no one asked him to go on a message. Some of his schoolmates even laughed at his new sign. Mr Gizenga, one of the neighbours, saw it and looked down under his glasses at the bike. With a ghost of a smile on his face, he said through his nose, 'I see, Charlie, you're on your way to your first million.'

But Charlie had the last laugh, because one day the business took off. Charlie was on his way home from school. Mr Lambe, the supermarket manager, called out, 'Hey, you boy!' He was standing at the back door of the shop, at the goods entrance.

Charlie went to him. The man was clearly upset. He didn't have his mobile phone, and a supermarket manager without his mobile phone is like a bird on one wing. Mr Lambe wanted Charlie to collect his mobile phone from a phone fixer in Chapel Lane.

'That will be fifty pence, Mr Lambe,' Charlie said.

'That's fine,' Mr Lambe said. 'Only hurry, please.'

Charlie put his head down and pedalled like mad towards Chapel Lane. The fixer had the phone ready, and Charlie was back in the supermarket in less than ten minutes.

'Well done!' said Mr Lambe. 'Here's a pound – and you can keep the change. Now, call in after school every day and I might have something for you to do. A bike is better than the van for short runs in heavy traffic.'

And so the CH Courier Service was in business. Mr Lambe got Charlie to run errands on several afternoons each week. People who did business with the supermarket got to know him, and they got him to fetch and carry for themselves.

Charlie's dad fitted two wire baskets behind the saddle, one on each side for balance. Everything was going fine. Charlie had a tin box under his bed and it was filling up with coins and bank notes. He was able to help out when cash was scarce at home. At the same time his own secret treasure was growing by the day.

But, as with all growing businesses, a time comes when improvements have to be made, and improvements cost money.

CH COURIERS EXPANDS

Old Mrs Dunne in High Street called him one day. 'I was looking for you yesterday,' she said. 'I can't walk too far with my arthritis and I wanted some food for Calypso.' Calypso was her three-legged dog – a truck had removed most of the left hind leg.

Charlie had been thinking about that problem already, before Mrs Dunne spoke to him. His business needed a phone. But they couldn't afford a phone. Charlie did what he usually did when he had a problem. He went to Miko Flanagan to talk about it.

'There's a phone here,' Miko said, 'but I'm not here to answer it all the time. I have to be out and around, buying and selling.'

'Why don't you get an office clerk?' Charlie asked.

'Can't,' Miko said. 'Not enough coming in to pay a clerk.'

Charlie thought about it for a minute. 'I have an idea,' he said at last, and he ran out the door of the hut before Miko could say another word.

Less than half an hour later Charlie was back again.

'I have a clerk for you,' he told Miko.

'I told you,' Miko said impatiently. 'I can't afford one.'

'You could afford this one, Miko; she would only be part time – just after school. And she wouldn't be too dear.'

'Who is she?'

Charlie opened the door and shouted, 'Minnie, come in!'

Minnie came in and stood before the desk. Charlie introduced her.

'She's a bit young,' said Miko.

'She's very clever and good at doing things,' Charlie said.

'I can talk for myself, Charlie,' Minnie said. Then she turned to Miko. 'I can answer your phone for you, Mister Flanagan. I answer the phone at home all the time. And I could write down all the phone messages that come in.'

'That would be okay for me,' Miko said, 'but Charlie here would need to be in touch more often. People usually want him at once.'

'He could phone in from a phone box and I'd give him his messages.'

In the end they agreed that she could work as their office clerk after school every day.

'What about my wages?' Minnie asked.

'How much do you think you're worth?' Miko asked.

'Two pounds a day for Monday to Friday and four pounds for Saturday because I'll be here Saturday morning as well.'

'Can we afford that, Charlie?' Miko asked Charlie.

Charlie shook his head. 'If we went half and half, maybe I could, but it wouldn't be right. Some days there might not be even one phone call and she would be getting money for doing nothing.'

Minnie raised her chin and said haughtily, 'I'd have to be here, wouldn't I? Surely I should be paid for being a prisoner here for a whole afternoon.'

'You'd be doing your homework or something,' Charlie said, 'and you'd be doing that if you never came in here.'

Minnie just turned and walked out the door.

Miko laughed. 'I like tough young ones,' he said to Charlie. 'Call her back.'

Minnie came back when Charlie called from the door.

'Maybe we could make some kind of a deal,' Miko said.

After a lot of arguing they came to an agreement. Minnie would get five pounds for being there for the week and three pence for every phone message delivered.

Both Miko and Charlie soon found out that it was well worth the money to have someone in the office at all times. Minnie kept a record of all the phone calls answered and before each entry she put C or M to show whether the call had been for Miko or Charlie.

MINNIE IS A TREASURE

Charlie was always on the move. At first it was tiring, but he got used to it. He could be seen every afternoon and all day on Saturdays pedalling furiously around the town, fetching and carrying for shops and private houses. He did the shopping for many old people and he delivered for several shops.

The sign on his bike had another line, giving Miko's phone number. Now it read: 'CH Courier Service, Phone 294692.

Minnie thought that people wouldn't have time to take down the number when he was flying past on the bike, so she suggested that he should put a note through the letter boxes around the town.

One afternoon when Charlie returned to the office, Minnie had the note worked out.

SAVE YOUR SHOE LEATHER
Let CH Courier Service run your errands
CH will carry anything from A to B
Fast and Reliable
From 3.30 p.m. to 6.00 p.m. Monday to Friday
10.00 a.m. to 6.00 p.m. on Saturdays
Phone 294692

Minnie agreed to write five hundred sheets by hand while in the office. She demanded a penny for each sheet. Charlie wanted to have it done for free. After all, she was doing it while they were paying her five pounds for just being there. In the end she agreed to do the whole lot for three pounds.

Things were going well. Charlie was very busy every afternoon. He phoned Minnie whenever he had an idle moment, and usually there was a message waiting for him to send him speeding to some other part of town on another errand.

At home the cash box was overflowing, and he had to change his coins to paper money. Mr Lambe in the supermarket was happy to change the money for him. He was always short of coins for his tills.

BIKES HAVE FEELINGS TOO

At night, when he put the bike in the shed, Charlie clipped on the walkman and had a good-night chat with Tiger.

'I hope I'm not working you too hard,' Charlie said after a very busy afternoon.

'No,' Tiger said. 'I like being on the move. It's a damn sight better than rusting away in a heap of cast-off metal in Miko Flanagan's yard.'

'That's good,' Charlie said. 'This courier business means a lot to me. I can buy a few things for myself and I'm able to help out while Dad and Mam are out of work.'

'But it's taking over your life, Charlie. You haven't time to talk to your friends any more.' Tiger sounded a little hurt.

'I talk to you, Tiger, every evening.'

'Yes, just for a few minutes, and then you're gone. You come in from school next day and you're in too much of a hurry to say a word. All you want to do is get out on those streets and pedal like mad around the town!'

'That's what I have to do,' Charlie said. 'Have you a problem with that?'

'I have. You're changing, and I don't like the new Charlie too much.'

'And what's wrong with the new Charlie?'

'He's getting greedy.'

'No, I'm not,' Charlie said, and he sounded cross.

'Okay, okay!' the bike said. 'Don't blow a gasket. I'm only telling you what I see. Where is all this going to end? When will you have enough?'

'Never!' Charlie said. 'I want to keep this going until I'm old enough to make it into a big business with vans and trucks and radio links and everything a big courier and haulage business needs.'

'Then you'll need another bike. I'm old and those parts you transplanted on to me are not in the best of shape. We're going to wear out soon from all this going.'

'Stop talking like that,' Charlie said. 'Without you there wouldn't be any business. You'll always be part of it. You're my mate, my partner.'

'So you say,' Tiger said. 'But I can see the day when I'm back in Flanagan's yard, waiting to be sold to the steel factory for recycling. I'll end up a molten spot in a huge ingot, my speech silent for ever, my thinking parts melted, and their atoms scattered.'

Charlie was silent for a while. He hadn't realised that Tiger had feelings like a person. To him the bike was only a thing, a talking thing without mind or heart. It was a machine that he was using to do the job it was made for, carrying him around the town.

'I promise you, Tiger,' he said at last. 'You'll never again be in a scrapheap. I'll never part with you.'

DISASTER!

For weeks after that talk Charlie was kinder to
Tiger. He rode it slowly, more like someone out
for a spin than a frenzied biker. He talked to it
more and they became closer friends.

One day Charlie was in Lambe's
supermarket. Mr Lambe gave him two bags of
groceries for an old woman who lived down
Featherdrop Lane. The bags were heavy, and
Charlie was thinking that they would balance
each other nicely in the two wire baskets.

When he came out the front door of the
supermarket, he stopped dead. The bike
wasn't where he had put it. He searched. It
wasn't anywhere else either. It was gone!

Charlie ran back into the shop. 'My bike is
gone!' he said to Mr Lambe.

Mr Lambe came to the door with him and
they searched in front of the shop and at the

back. No sign of the bike! Mr Lambe sent for the police.

The squad car came and Garda Quinn asked Charlie about the bike. What make was it and which model? Charlie tried to explain what the bike looked like, and told them that it was a bike made up of bits and pieces of different makes.

'Have you the number?' Garda Quinn asked.

'What number?' Charlie asked.

'There's always a number,' the garda said. 'It's usually engraved on the frame, just under the saddle.'

'If it was an old frame it might be somewhere else,' his colleague said.

'If it was before 1966, it could,' Garda Quinn agreed. 'It could be anywhere on the frame. Sometimes it was so small you'd have a job to find it.'

They wrote down all the details and went

away. They said they would do all they could to find it.

In the meantime Charlie was grounded. He had to work on foot. He soon found out that this was no good. He couldn't get around to as many places as when he had the bike. He was forced to rent a bike from Moone's second-hand bicycle shop.

Two pounds a day the bike rent cost him. When he had paid that and given Minnie her wages and paid for his phone messages, he had little enough left for himself. The heap of money in the cash box was growing at a snail's pace. Several times he thought of giving it all up. Without Tiger it was hardly worth the effort.

The rented bike did the job okay, but Tiger's saddle had become worn to the shape of his bottom and he and the old bike were comrades. The rented bike had no personality, and it was silent as a stone.

Charlie thought he would have to save his money for a new bike. He began to read ads in The Evening Gazette for bikes. They came under 'Cycles', and were mostly for second-hand bikes, but there were ads also for a few shops selling new models. Charlie read them all, but he didn't find anything to suit him. They were either too old or too dear.

BICYCLE THIEVES

One Friday evening Charlie called to the scrapyard to give Minnie her week's wages. Miko was there.

'Could you come early tomorrow morning, Charlie?' Miko asked.

'What for?' Charlie asked.

'I want to take some stuff to the dump, car seats and old tyres and used batteries that are of no use to anyone. They're only taking up space here. I want a hand to throw them out of the van.'

Charlie and Miko drove to the dump early the following morning. The sun was peeping over the roofs and chimneys of Brown Street. The town was only waking up.

At the dump they pulled in beside a

yellow van with the words Acme Cycle Store in black. Charlie stood at the back door of Miko's van and he and Miko began to throw the stuff over the low wall.

Charlie stopped and shouted to Miko, 'Look, Miko!'

'Look where?' Miko said.

'Look! Look! Down there!'

Miko looked down at the pile of rubbish – hedge clippings, rotten timber, bags of domestic refuse, pots, an old television set, a computer screen and bits of old bikes. Sitting on top of the heap were two wire baskets and a metal plate with the words CH Courier Service.

'What am I looking for?' Miko said.

'Look there,' Charlie said, pointing. 'My baskets and my sign. There they are!'

'So they are!' said Miko slowly. 'So they are, and they're on top. Those boys beside us there must have thrown them away.'

'I'll ask them where they got them,' Charlie said, and he was about to step around the side of the van, but the other van was pulling away from the wall.

'Let them go,' Miko said.

'Why? They had my baskets and they're getting away.'

'Calm down, Charlie. There's no point in asking them. They'll just tell you lies. There are other ways of dealing with them.'

'But they're getting away, Miko.'

'They won't be going far. I know where their place is in New Street. Down by the Bank of Ireland. We might give them a call later today.'

ROBBERS' LAIR

After lunch Miko's van pulled up outside the
Acme Cycle Store in New Street, and he and
Charlie went in. A woman and a man were
attending to some customers.

'I'll be with you in a tick,' the man said to
them, so Miko and Charlie had to wait. They
rambled around the shop, looking at the
bikes, all new and shining.

'What can I do for you?' a voice said in
Charlie's ear. It was the woman, and she
looked Miko up and down and sniffed as if
she were worried about the good name of
her shop. He had his scrapyard clothes on
and he hadn't bothered to clean the black
from his face.

'I'm looking for a bike for this young
man,' Miko told her.

'Have you seen anything you'd like?'

'We'd like them all. Isn't that right, Charlie?' Miko said, smiling his big white smile in his oil-black face.

'Well, then, have you picked one out?' she asked, and Charlie could see that she wanted to get rid of them as quickly as she could.

'They're too dear for us,' Miko said looking at the price tag on one beside him. 'Two hundred and thirty-nine pounds!' he said and he laughed politely. 'Enough for a small car – second-hand, that is.'

'Second-hand,' the woman said quickly. 'Through that door at the back.' And she was gone. Charlie watched her stiff back move down the avenue between the gleaming handlebars.

The back was a large concrete yard with a small office and a workshop at one end. They could hear the clink of metal on metal in the workshop, and through the office window they saw a youngish man with a lot of black hair bunched on top of his head and lumped about his ears.

Miko knocked at the office door, and a voice shouted a long, drawn-out, 'Y-e-ss!' They went in. The man with the hair was at a desk near the window, looking over a ledger and scribbling figures on scraps of paper which he tore up and threw in a waste-paper basket beside him.

Miko leaned on the short counter and said, 'Second-hand bikes?'

'What about second-hand bikes?' said The Hair, without looking up from his ledger.

'What kind of price are we talking about?' Miko asked.

'We're not talking about a price,' The Hair answered. He closed the ledger and came to the counter. 'Now, if you were serious about buying a bike, then we might be talking about a price.'

'Good!' said Miko. 'At last you're getting tuned in. We'll know if we're serious about buying a bike when we see one.'

'The shed beyond the workshop,' the man said, and he went back to his sums.

They had to pass the workshop on the way to the shed. The door was closed and the only window was high. The sound of someone working on metal had stopped and there was a sawing sound.

'Take a peep,' said Miko and he lifted Charlie up to the window. He held him there for just a second, and took him down again.

'Did he see you?' Miko asked.

'No. His back was turned. I think he has a stolen bike,' Charlie said.

'How do you know it was stolen?' Miko asked. 'I hope your imagination isn't running away with you.'

'He was sawing through a lock on a bike. Is that a give-away or what?'

'Maybe he lost the key.'

'Miko!'

'Okay, okay. Now we know,' Miko said in a whisper, 'but we must move like we were walking on eggs. Come on, let's see if your bike is there.'

McGILLICUDDY LENDS A HAND

They went into the shed. It was a huge shed with bike-stands full of old bikes, some not so old and others ancient. At one end they found about ten bikes that were mongrels, bits of different makes put together to make workable bikes.

'If Tiger is anywhere, he's here,' Charlie said.

'They must have changed the colours,' Miko said. 'No sign of your black and yellow stripes.'

In the end they found Tiger. At least Charlie was sure it was Tiger, in spite of its new coat of black paint. The saddle was a give-away: no other bike in the world could have a saddle worn to that precise pattern of hills and valleys. It was priced at twenty-five pounds.

'It's no use,' Miko said. 'We must be sure, and we must be able to say for definite that it is your bike. We must be able to prove it.'

'How can we do that?'

'I don't know. I'll have to ask Murt.'

'Who?'

'Murt McGillicuddy. He's a guard, and he's a friend. Come on. We'll come back after lunch.'

Miko put his head in the office door and said, 'There's a few of them there we like. They're the right price too. I've no money on me now, but we'll come back later and we might do a deal.'

Murt McGillicuddy was on office duty when they called to the Garda station.

'We've been keeping an eye on those fellows,' he told Miko. 'Bikes have been disappearing all over the place lately, and that Acme outfit has an awful lot of second-hand bikes for sale.'

'Why don't ye ask them some questions?' Charlie asked. He knew from television programmes that police always solved crimes by asking questions.

'No good asking questions unless we have a bit of evidence.'

'Like what?' Charlie asked.

'Like the number on the bike.'

'Tell me about the number,' Charlie said. 'I'd like to hear it again.'

Guard McGillicuddy was patient. 'Don't you know,' he said, 'every bike has a number engraved on the frame. If we knew the number of a stolen bike we could maybe find out who owned it.'

When they got back to the scrapyard office, Charlie said, 'They're on again about numbers. I don't know anything about a number. I never saw a number on Tiger and

I painted every bit of it.'

'Not every bit,' Minnie said. 'Remember, I painted some of it.'

'Did you see a number?' Miko asked her.

'I did,' she said, 'just under the saddle on the frame.'

'Come on, Minnie,' Charlie said impatiently, 'what was it?'

'I don't remember,' Minnie answered. 'I didn't know what it meant. All I can remember is that there was a seven in it, and, oh yes, a two, and – and maybe a one.'

'No use,' Miko said. 'We'd have to be sure. Is there anything at all you can do, Charlie, to find out which of those old bikes it might be?'

Charlie thought for a while. 'If only I could talk to it,' he said without thinking.

'Now you've really flipped your lid,' Miko said. 'Maybe you'd like to have a word with my old van as you're at it!'

Minnie laughed. 'You're joking, of course.'

'Only in a way,' Charlie said, trying to cover up for spilling his secret. 'You see, when I look over the bike and see what I can tell about it by the way it looks, it's the same as if it talked to me.'

Charlie looked at Miko, and he could see questions in the man's eyes, but they were not asked out loud.

'What I'm really saying,' Charlie said, 'is that I'd like a few minutes alone to examine the bike.'

'Okay,' Miko said, 'if that's what you want.'

A PALINDROME

When they went back to the Acme Cycle
Store, Miko went into the office and began to
argue about the price of the bike. Charlie, in
the meantime, slipped into the shed.

He took out his walkman and clipped it
to the handlebars of the bike he identified
as Tiger. It spoke to him clear as a lark on a
calm day.

'About time you got here! Take me out
of this wretched place. In here with a
crowd of dummies! Not a word out of any
of them.'

Charlie explained that he couldn't take
him without being able to prove that it was
his bike. He told Tiger what Garda
McGillicuddy said – about the number to
identify him.

'Well then, tell him about the number,' said Tiger.

'I didn't see a number on you,' Charlie said.

'How could you? You were too busy slapping paint on me. Your friend, Minnie, saw it though.'

'Okay, tell me the number.'

'What number?'

'The number I didn't see when I was slapping paint on you.'

'Oh, that number! 0711428.'

'Thank you. I'll tell the garda.'

'Won't do you much good.'

'Why not?'

'They filed it off.'

Charlie was cross. 'Then why did you tell it to me?' he shouted.

'You asked me.'

'Okay,' Charlie said. 'So you don't have a number now.'

'I do,' said Tiger. 'They engraved a new number on me.'

'Well, come on! Are you going to keep it a secret?'

'It's 717717. Easy to remember. It's a palindrome.'

Charlie went to the door of the office. Miko was leaning across the counter, talking to The Hair. The Hair wasn't really listening to him. He was seated at a computer, flicking at the keys and staring at the screen. Charlie winked at Miko and beckoned him away.

He told Miko what he knew.

'How did you find out?' Miko asked.

'I have ways,' Charlie said.

'You're a mystery man,' Miko said. 'I suppose now you expect me to believe that you have some magic powers?'

'I don't care what you believe,' Charlie said.

'Oh, oh, touch me not! Let's get out of here,' Miko said. 'We have to talk to Murt.'

Murt called the sergeant when they told him that Charlie knew the number of the stolen bike. The sergeant got a form for missing property and filled it out. He wrote the number 717717 in the space for identifying marks. When he had it completed, Charlie signed it.

They drove to the bicycle shop in a garda car, Charlie and Miko in the back and Murt McGillicuddy and Sergeant Tom Burke in front. Murt drove.

I HATE VIOLENCE

Sergeant Burke walked into the office, and said, 'We have come to enquire about a stolen bicycle. Will you show us your stock of second-hand bikes, please.' Charlie was amused when he saw the look of open-eyed shock on The Hair's face.

But The Hair got over his surprise quickly. 'Certainly,' he said. 'Please follow me.'

He led them towards the shed. As they passed the workshop, the sergeant asked, 'What's in there?'

'Oh, that's just the workshop,' The Hair answered casually, as if it didn't matter.

'Take a look in there,' the sergeant told Murt.

Murt asked Miko to go with him, because

he would know what went on in a workshop. In the meantime, the sergeant followed The Hair to the shed, and Charlie went with them.

'Have a look at the bikes and see if yours is among them,' the sergeant said to Charlie.

Charlie knew where his bike was, but he walked up and down, examining all the bikes before he put his hand on Tiger and said, 'That's my bike.'

'Where did you get that bike?' the sergeant asked The Hair.

'I'll have to look it up in the computer,' The Hair said and they went back to the office. The Hair went to the computer and fiddled with the keyboard. He looked at the screen, and said, 'We got that in a sale of old bikes in a cycle shop that was closing down in Sheffield in England.'

'Oh, yes?' the sergeant said. 'And I suppose the shop is now closed down and

there is no way of contacting the former owners.'

'I think that would be accurate,' The Hair said.

'You must think I'm a complete fool,' Sergeant Burke said. 'I've heard that story before. We have reason to believe that bike was taken from in front of Lambe's supermarket.'

'How could you possibly think that?' The Hair said.

'Easy enough to check,' the sergeant said, and he drew Charlie's missing-property form from his pocket. 'If the number on this form matches the number on the bike, you're for a holiday behind bars. Let's go out and see.'

When they discovered that the numbers were identical, The Hair stood there with his mouth open for a few seconds.

'That's impossible. It couldn't be,' he muttered. 'We replaced —'

He put his hand to his mouth, knowing that he had just blown the whistle on himself. When he realised that the game was up, he bolted, and ran towards the door, but Murt McGillicuddy and Miko had come from the workshop, and Murt was standing, a great navy-blue square blocking the doorway.

'Please, young man, don't try to run past me,' Murt pleaded. 'I hate violence.'

The sergeant placed his hand on The Hair's shoulder and said: 'I am arresting you on a charge of theft. You are not obliged to say anything, but anything you do say may be taken down and used as evidence in your trial, if this matter should come to trial.'

Then the sergeant turned to Murt. 'Place his accomplice under arrest, Guard McGillicuddy,' he said.

BACK TO NORMAL

The Hair and his accomplice, the one who did the work on the stolen bikes, were taken to the police station and formally charged. The people in the Acme Cycle Store were not involved. They rented the back yard and sheds to the others to trade in second-hand bicycles. They knew nothing of what was going on.

In a short time Charlie and Tiger were reunited. Charlie was once again to be seen in the afternoons, cycling at speed around the streets and lanes of the town.

One evening Charlie sat on the ground beside Tiger in the shed at the back of the house. The clip was on the handlebars, and the earphones were in place.

'I nearly lost you,' Charlie said. 'Only for

seeing the sign and the baskets at the dump you were gone for ever.'

'You should have had a lock on me,' Tiger said.

'I didn't think anyone would be bothered,' Charlie said.

'Oh, thank you very much,' Tiger said, and Charlie knew that he had made a terrible mistake. Tiger was insulted.

'You're very touchy,' Charlie said. 'I didn't mean that the way you think. How was I to know you'd be kidnapped by professional robbers? I knew that no young one would steal you with that sign on you. They wouldn't do it because they'd know they'd be spotted at once.'

'You're not just saying that to butter me up?'

'No. No. You know I'm not,' Charlie assured him. 'We're mates, aren't we?'

'Good,' said Tiger, and he sounded happy

again. Although he knew all the secrets of the world, in some ways he was very innocent.

'Things are back to normal, then,' he said.

'With me running a business with a talking bicycle as a partner,' Charlie said. He turned away from Tiger and raised his eyebrows. 'Yes. I suppose we could call that "normal".'

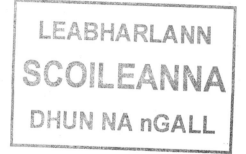

ALSO BY FRANK MURPHY

LOCKIE AND DADGE
Frank Murphy

Winner of a Bisto Book of the Year Merit Award and the Eilís Dillon Memorial Award 1996, this is Frank's first book. Lockie is a bit of a misfit. Orphaned, he is placed in foster home after foster home, but somehow he never settles in. Finally, he runs away, and meets up with some colourful characters – Dadge and his strange friends Pasha and Mammy Tallon. For the first time Lockie doesn't feel like an outsider. But others are out to wreck his happiness.

OTHER BOOKS FROM THE O'BRIEN PRESS

ADAM'S STARLING
Gillian Perdue

Adam's Starling tells the story of a nine-year-old boy who is finding life difficult. At home, no-one has any time for him. At school things are even worse – a gang of bullies has singled him out for punishment. But then a scruffy little starling comes into Adam's life. This is Adam's secret, his own special friend. But can he defend his small friend against the bullies? Will he find the courage he has needed all along?

WOLFGRAN
Finbar O'Connor

A sequel to the story of Little Red Riding Hood, Wolfgran is a wonderfully irreverent take on the world of fairy tales. Granny has moved to a retirement home but the Big Bad Wolf is still on her trail! Disguised as a little old lady, 'Wolfgran' is causing mayhem as he prowls the city streets, swallowing anybody who gets in his way. Hot on his case are Chief Inspector Plonker, who thinks he has a werewolf on his hands, Sergeant Snoop, who has to melt down his darts' trophy to make silver bullets, and a very clever little girl guide in a red hood. But will they get to the wolf before he gets Granny? And who will let all those little old ladies out of their cells in time for bingo?

WOLFGRAN RETURNS
Finbar O'Connor

Inspector Plonker is once more on the trail of his old enemy, Wolfgran, but this time he's going undercover. Disguised in a pantomime wolf suit, can the Inspector and his faithful sidekick Sergeant Snoop escape being throttled by Granny Riding Hood's nephew, blasted by the Chief of Police, hand-bagged by a bus queue full of very cranky old ladies and run over by the terrifying vets from TV's 'Pet Patrol'?

And will they manage to stop the Big Bad Wolf before he gets to the Grand Gala Bingo Night and finally makes a meal of Little Red Riding Hood?

WALTER SPEAZLEBUD
David Donohue

Walter Speazlebud is a whizz at spelling backwards. While the other children in his class struggle to remember their spellings *forwards*, Walter can rattle off any word *backwards*. But Walter has an even better gift: the power of Noitanigami (imagination). That means he can make people, and animals, go backwards in time. Walter inherited both skills from his favourite person: his grandfather. So when his horrible teacher, Mr Strong, starts picking on Walter, he had better watch out. And so had the even more horrible class bully, Danny Biggles. Because when Speazlebud's about, it spells elbuort (trouble) for all bullies ...

Send for our full-colour catalogue or check out our website